Magical Mayhem

Part Seven

To Prevent Fresh Starts

Emily Martha Sorensen

Also by Emily Martha Sorensen

Wicked Witches of Restva:
Black Magic Academy

Fairy Senses:
Fairy Eyeglasses
Fairy Compass
Fairy Earmuffs
Fairy Barometer
Fairy Pox
Fairy Slippers
Fairy Lunchbox
Fairy Icepack
Fairy Stopwatch
Fairy Toothbrush
Fairy Perfume

Dragon Eggs:
Dragon's Egg
Dragon's Hope
Dragon's First Christmas
Dragon's Fire
Dragon's Song

Comics:
A Magical Roommate
To Prevent World Peace

Picture Books:
Tabby, Tabby, Burning Bright

The End in the Beginning:
The Keeper and the Rulership
The Fires of the Rulership
The Magic or the Rulership

Trilogy of a Teenage Werevulture:
Trials of a Teenage Werevulture
Trifles of a Teenage Werevulture
Weredodo Sleuth

The Numbers Just Keep
Getting Bigger:
Twenty-Four Potential
Children of Prophecy

Not Quite a Harem:
Not Quite a Curse

Magical Mayhem:
To Prevent World Peace
To Prevent Chic Costumes
To Prevent Clear Paths
To Prevent Smart Choices
To Prevent Warm Welcomes
To Prevent Cute Mascots
To Prevent First Place (prologue)

Short Story Collections:
Worlds of Wonder
Magic and Mischief

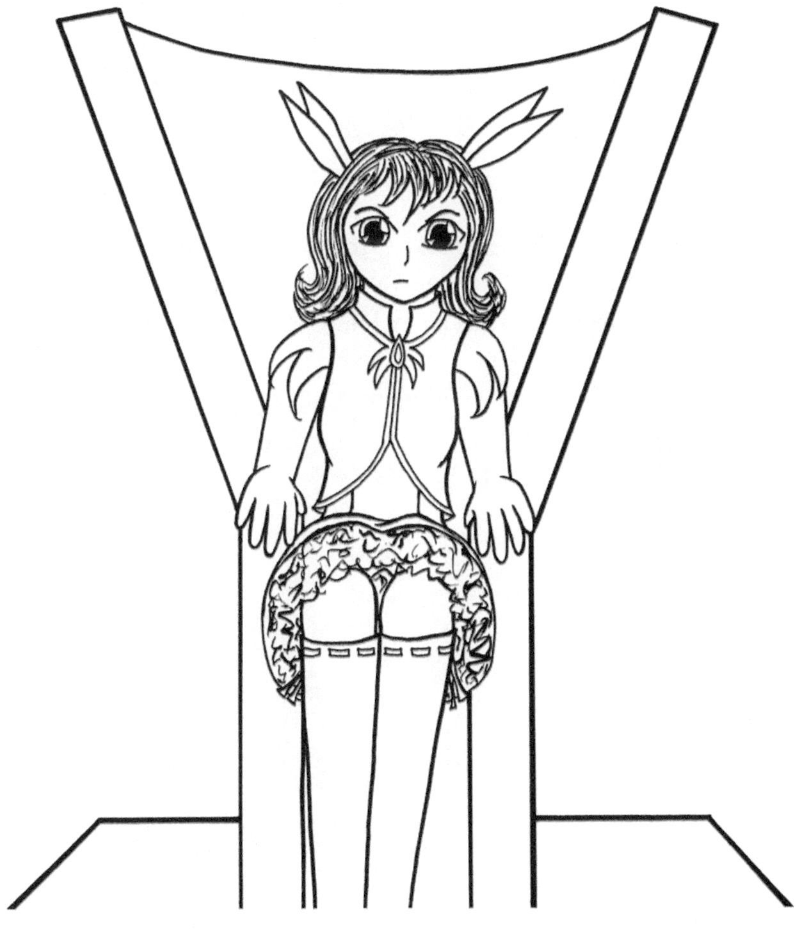

To Prevent Fresh Starts

Magical Mayhem Part #7: To Prevent Fresh Starts
Copyright © 2018 by Emily Martha Sorensen
Cover and internal art by Emily Martha Sorensen

ISBN: 978-1-949607-27-7

http://www.emilymarthasorensen.com

To Frederik Vendelin,

longtime fan of the comic,
reader of my other books,
and Patreon supporter.

Chapter 1
The Basics

Empty seats stretched out in front of them in vast rows. Florence and her family were being allowed to preboard the airplane because they were the special guests of the president of Mágico. They'd even been given first class seats.

"My private plane is all booked for the morning of the 19th," Presidente Eloise Santos's letter had said apologetically, *"but that would be the best time for you to travel here, as I have an empty space in my schedule that afternoon. Would you be willing to travel by commercial jet instead? If so, I can arrange for you to have complimentary first class seats on our national airline."*

When Florence had opened that letter, she'd stared at it in shock. *Presidente Santos wants to have someone meet with me? Me?! The president of an entire country?!*

This after spending three months trying to get the attention of a single person back home. No one had listened to her explanation about why a magical girl government was necessary, and some of the groups she'd presented her ideas to had laughed. One man had even, insultingly, told her, "Sweetheart, if you want to run this thing to get more rights for magical girls, try graduating from high school first."

Talk about completely missing the point!

First of all, she hadn't been talking about trying to get more rights for magical girls, she'd been talking about the need for more oversight, which was practically the opposite.

And second, she'd never said she wanted to run it! All she wanted was for this organization to exist. After that, she'd be happy to fade back into the background and resume normal life again. Of course she wasn't qualified to run something like a worldwide bureaucracy! Duh!

But when her father had written to the ambassador of Mágico, they had gotten an unbelievable personal response filled with enthusiasm, taking the idea perfectly seriously.

Not from the ambassador her father had written to. Oh, no.

From that country's *president.*

"I can't believe we're on an airplane," Florence whispered to herself, standing in the doorway and staring out at the vast, empty rows. "An *airplane!*"

She'd never flown in her life.

Well, no, that wasn't true. She'd flown under her own power, of course, with Pink Dragon's bat wings. But flying on an airplane, miles and miles up in the sky? It was unbelievable. Airplanes were something for rich people, and her family was hardly rich. Her father was a pastor.

She'd never been out of the country before, much less to a different continent. Sure, there were magical girls who got invited to travel to other worlds to save civilizations of mascots, but her team had never been one of them. The farthest Florence had ever traveled was a ten-hour drive to see her grandmother, still in the same state.

And now they were flying to South America to visit *Terra de Liberdade e Mágica,* a.k.a. "Land of Liberty and Magic," called Mágico for short. It was famous for being the country with the highest concentration of magical girls in the world.

Well, unless you counted Antarctica, which needed magical girls to keep the climate temperate within its settlements.

Or Moon Base, whose bubble cities required magical girls to keep air circulating.

But neither of those places was a country in its own right. They were both Australian colonies. Mágico was its own country. Every nation but Brazil, which they'd broken off from, recognized that. It was a new country, only five years old, but it was already famous for its odd and nonstandard ways of doing things.

Such as, say, allowing ten-year-olds to vote and run for public office.

And holding new presidential elections every year.

And requiring one of the presidential candidates to be a current or past magical girl.

And having no standing military, just a defense grid comprised entirely of volunteer magical girls.

Yeah, by any standards, Mágico was *weird*.

"Welcome to Liberdade Airlines!" a woman called out to them, beckoning them to their seats. "I'll be your hostess on this trip!"

Florence tried very hard not to flinch at the woman's outfit. It wasn't that it was inappropriate . . . for a five-year-old. But a grown woman in her thirties should not be wearing quite so many hearts and ruffles, nor quite so much pink.

"Does Mágico have magical girls your age?" Florence's father asked the woman as they followed her to their seats.

"Me? No, no," the woman laughed, waving at her costume. "I died in the revolution. This is the airline uniform."

You mean we're going to have to look at a whole bunch of middle-aged women dressed like that? Florence wanted to die.

"How old were you when you died?" Florence's mother asked politely.

"Mmm, my magical girl form got killed five years ago, so . . . twenty-four?"

Florence's father looked shocked. "That's still very old for a magical girl. Most lose their powers before they turn eighteen. How did you manage it?"

The woman laughed. "Oh, well, they say the better a person you are, the longer you can keep your powers, you know. Of course, that sounds like bragging," she added mischievously. "So it was probably just that I didn't believe I *had* to lose them."

"Does that make a difference?" Florence's mother asked.

"Of course it does!" The woman looked startled. "If you don't think you're worthy anymore, or if you think you're too old, you'll lose your magic even if you'd otherwise be eligible to keep it. Don't you know the basics?"

"Apparently I don't," Florence's father murmured, looking very thoughtful.

"Oh, well, just think of it like a contract," the woman said, waving her hand. "Both the girl and the magic system have to agree that she's eligible. Boys can't become magical girls because the magic system doesn't consent. Girls who think they can't have magic can't be magical girls because *they* don't consent. That's why only girls who believed in magic already were able to become magical girls in the first generation, you know? Both sides have to agree. And if either side stops consenting, then the magic leaves."

"What if a girl believes she's wicked, even though she isn't?" Florence's father asked slowly.

Florence knew who he meant. He meant Kendra, her best friend who was now a villain because she'd listened to some born mage's crazy sales pitch about magical girls destroying the world. For some reason, her best friend had decided it would be a good idea to go become an outlaw instead of founding a legal organization to stop the problem, which was such an obviously superior solution. Argh, Florence got so frustrated thinking about it!

"Same thing," the woman in the embarrassing uniform said, shrugging. "If a girl doesn't think she's good enough for magic, she can't be a magical girl, even if she wants to. You see it all the time with girls who have low self-esteem. It's a pity. My niece, for instance . . ."

But Florence was only half-listening. She already knew all that. It was one of the points she made in her presentation, in fact: young people with high self-esteem were the most likely segment of the population to overestimate their own virtue.

As she took her aisle seat across from her parents, sitting next to a man by the window, she summoned her bracelet. It appeared on her wrist with a roar of flame.

The Basics

The man beside her looked startled. He had longish grey hair and was balding at the temples. "Are you a magical girl?"

"Um . . ." Florence hesitated. *Good question.* "I don't know. I *was* one."

Now he looked puzzled. "How can you not know?"

"Well, I was thinking about quitting . . ." Florence hedged. "I wasn't entirely sure if I wanted to, but I was sure I didn't want to be Pink Dragon anymore. And then *this* happened."

She gestured at her forearm. Her focus item had changed shape three months ago, immediately after she had started talking to her parents about starting the Sonnenkinder Government. It was no longer a thick bracelet with three gemstones on it. Now it was a long, thin spiral that covered her entire forearm, and there were twelve gems on it.

Twelve.

Each of those three gems had given her a different power while transformed. In theory, this meant she now ought to have twelve powers. Except she hadn't been able to transform at all since the bracelet's mutation.

In more morbid moments, it reminded her of the way Kendra's halo had grown spikes right before she'd run off to be a villain. But, thankfully, those extra gemstones weren't spikes. They seemed more like a typical magical girl power-up.

At her first power-up, Florence had gone from having one gem and one power to having three gems and three powers. Those twelve gems seemed like a logical extension of what had happened two years ago. Theoretically, she should be powered up and have nine more powers than before.

Which would be great, if only she could transform and figure out what they *did.*

Am I blocking myself from transforming? Florence wondered, looking at the woman in the embarrassing costume, who was still chattering with her parents while they took their seats across the aisle and next to Florence. *Do I think I'm not worthy, or something?*

As far as she could tell, she didn't think she wasn't worthy. She definitely didn't think she was too old.

Maybe she didn't want to be a magical girl anymore? But in that case, her focus item would have crumbled because she was quitting.

Besides, she *did* want to be a magical girl. The idea of having a fresh start, of remaking herself all over again, was exciting. It was exactly what she needed, now that her team was gone. Imagining a new costume that wasn't pink and fluffy, new powers to play with, no Kendra telling her what to do . . .

She wasn't sure what she wanted for her new magical girl form, only what she didn't want. And that was exactly why she was so eager to transform and find out how it had changed. Magical girl forms always reflected who you wanted to be. Once she saw what she had, she'd understand what she wanted.

If only her transformation would work.

"So what are you going to Mágico for?" the man beside her asked with a faint accent, snapping Florence out of her brooding.

"Oh . . . I'm trying to start a government for magical girls," she said offhandedly.

The man blinked. "A what now?"

"A government for magical girls. You know, so that we have more oversight and accountability."

The man looked puzzled. "Doesn't Mágico already have one of those?"

Florence shook her head. "Not a government *of* magical girls, a government *for* magical girls."

"The Mágico government isn't all magical girls," the man said. "The president before Eloise Santos was a former military leader named Rafael Bianchi. He served for a year before she was elected, you know."

"Yes, whatever," Florence said, waving her hand. She'd never heard of the man. "Their first president was a magical girl, and their current president is a former magical girl. That's two out of three."

"Only because the country is five years old, and its population is wildly imbalanced in favor of teenage girls," the man said mildly. "In a decade, things will have shifted significantly."

Right, as if that mattered.

"In any case, why start a government for magical girls?" the man asked, folding his hands on his lap. "They're all citizens of their own countries, aren't they?"

"Yes, but it's way too easy to consider ourselves exempt from the laws of our countries, because the people enforcing them don't have magic," Florence explained.

The man looked puzzled. "Correct me if I'm wrong, but don't most countries allow magical girls to volunteer as law enforcement aides?"

"Not as many as you'd think," Florence said. "The U.S. and Canada do. So does Mágico. But there are some countries where magical girls are persecuted —"

"Like Brazil," the man said, nodding.

"— and some where they're conscripted into the military —"

"Like Japan and China."

"— and some where it's considered too dangerous to allow little girls to help the police, so the most they're allowed to do is help with community service —"

"Like Russia."

"— and some where the laws are way too lenient because they need magic to survive —"

"Like Antarctica."

The man was surprisingly well-informed.

"Anyway," Florence said quickly, "I'm going to Mágico to see someone about starting it. No one back home would listen to me. This time, though . . . I hope someone will."

"Who did you ask back home?" the man asked.

Florence sighed. "We tried contacting my old acquaintances in the police and the FBI. People I knew when I volunteered as a magical girl aide. When I told them what I wanted to accomplish, they looked at me funny. After that, I took it to a few nonprofits and international corporations. They just laughed at me. So I'm starting to feel all, 'Nothing's going to work,' and then Dad writes to the ambassador of Mágico, who writes to the president, who asks us to come and tells the ambassador to book flights for us . . . and so he sends for an airplane! First class seats, too!"

"Not very surprising," the man said with a wry smile. "Our current president is not known for being thrifty."

"Is she bad with money?" Florence asked, surprised.

"Mmm, not according to the voters, I suppose. They seem to think getting in debt to foreign nations is fine as long as it stimulates economic progress. Never mind that. Are you meeting with the president or someone else while you're there?"

"Oh, I'm sure it's someone else," Florence said. "The president is definitely way too busy."

"Really? Did she say that?" The man looked mildly interested. "It seems rather unlike her to delegate anything."

"She's the president of an entire nation," Florence explained, barely stopping herself from adding *duh*. "Just because I want to start a government for magical girls doesn't mean other governments are going to take it seriously before it gets off the ground. I just hope I'll be able to talk to someone high enough up to have the pull to help me organize it."

The woman in the embarrassing costume stopped chattering with Florence's parents and turned around. "Oh, are you the one starting the thing to help the *escondidas meninas*? That's so exciting!"

"*Escon . . .* what?" Florence repeated, baffled.

"*Escondidas meninas,*" the man beside her put in. Going back to English, he explained, with a faint Brazilian accent, "It means 'hidden girls.' It's been the term for magical girls in Brazil ever since magic was made illegal. We don't tend to use that term in Mágico, since we don't hide our magical girls there." He gave the woman a faint disapproving look.

She seemed blithely unaware, too focused on Florence to care. "Senhora Presidente is very excited to meet you! She wants to hear your proposal —"

"Wait." Florence's mind jammed. "I'm meeting the president of Mágico *personally?*"

"But of course!" the woman laughed. "We're a small country, you know? Not that much bureaucracy. And she's been looking for somebody with a vision like yours for *years!*"

Florence started to sweat. *I did* want somebody to take me seriously . . .

"Oh, Former President Bianchi!" the woman cried, looking at the man beside Florence. "I didn't realize you were going to be on this flight! How was your vacation?"

"Very restful, thanks," the man said, smiling.

Florence turned slowly, and looked at the man beside her in horror. The man who was, apparently, the previous president of *Terra de Liberdade e Mágica.*

He chuckled. "We are, as she said, a small country."

Florence wanted to die.

Chapter 2
The Lecture

Congratulations, minions!" Rhea announced, prancing into the classroom at the top floor above her store. "Your boss asked me to give you a few seminars on basic villainy!"

There was rustling and grumbling from the five brand new minions seated in uncomfortable chairs. They were all young men, between teens and early twenties, and all of them had been hired just recently.

Rhea's main business was, of course, making and selling costumes. But she also had a side business teaching lectures on basic villainy to minions. She'd started it back in the beginning because she'd needed the money, and she kept doing it now because she found it entertaining.

Rhea surveyed the minions' costumes with a professional eye. Even though she hadn't been hired to design them, she found them acceptable, despite them being cliche. It wasn't wholly bad for a minion to be unoriginal, after all. What mattered was for a minion to look clearly villainish, and these costumes did that.

One of them had spiked hair and wore all black, with his boss's logo splashed in yellow across the front of his sleeveless shirt. It was either blatant sucking up or a requirement from his boss, and either way, there was nothing wrong with it.

One of them wore copious quantities of fur, which looked a little bit too fluffy for Rhea's taste, but the fact that it was all from endangered animals was a nice, if slightly too subtle, touch.

One had a cloak with gemstones in a gold band around the collar. Sitting down, it didn't look like much, but if he was at all decent with swishing that thing, he might be able to look reasonably impressive.

One of them had spiked shoulderblades, a classic look. She would have had no problems with it save that he was a little too nondescript to pull it off; when wearing spiked shoulderblades, one should aim to look either desirably sexy or intimidatingly ugly. Anything in between showed you were a mere wannabe. Still, makeup could fix that.

The last one had the best costume of them all. The gigantic, stiff collar looked magnificently impressive beside his goatee. It might have been overboard on a clean-shaven man, but with that facial hair, the balance was excellent.

After one second of eyeing them and passing judgment on their costumes, Rhea turned to shut the door to the classroom behind her. Occasionally a nosy customer wandered upstairs, despite the sign saying "Employees Only," and it would be a nuisance to have to pretend these minions were attacking her.

Especially since the nosiest customers were usually magical girls. They had an irritating tendency to think being an emissary of love and justice meant they were justified in wandering anywhere they pleased to search for possible monsters of the week.

In any case, there was a reason there were three entrances to Rhea's store. One was the storefront for mainstream customers. One was for minions and villains to enter in secret, so that the Paris police wouldn't see wanted criminals frequenting Rhea's establishment. And one was a secret way in and out that only she knew about, in case of emergencies.

Whenever mainstream customers asked what was on the top floor of her store, Rhea casually lied and said that it was where she stored inventory. At one time, it had been exactly that. But she had little need to store inventory anymore.

Nor did she have a need to sew. Nor did she even need to make patterns, except in cases when Minerva was being particularly dense about interpreting how a sketched garment should be constructed.

Truly, Minerva was the best investment she had ever made in her business.

Rhea often heard boss villains complain about the incompetence of their minions, and to be sure, most minions were incompetent. That was a reason so many villains send their new hires to her to brush up on the fundamentals of villainy. It was astonishing how clueless some of them could be, joining only because of the mystique of villainy and the promise of extremely high wages . . . combined with absolutely no statistics about survival rates.

But the problem was, a minion who was too stupid to look up survival rates from other sources before leaping at the chance to join was a minion who was likely useless. And any minion that *was* reasonably clever would have no loyalty to the boss who had deceived them into joining.

The fact of the matter was, deceiving one's enemies was entertaining. Deceiving one's allies was exhausting. If you didn't have employees you could trust absolutely, your business was a house of cards, just waiting to collapse at the slightest breeze.

Rhea knew that better than most, seeing as she delighted in collapsing enemies or rivals with shaky foundations by putting pressure on the weakest links. She'd been doing that on behalf of her family since she was a child.

That was why Rhea had decided to hire only one employee, and she had waited to hire that one, despite desperately needing a minion for over a year, until she had found the perfect choice for the job.

Minerva.

Technically her minion's real name was Zazz, and it was fine for her to use that in villain circles, but Rhea had mandated that her employee use a public name that seemed reasonably plausible as belonging to their world. The same went for the tail: it was fine for her to show it around villains, but in public, it was necessary for her to not be obviously an illegal alien from another world.

The Lecture

Since her assistant had had no opinion about what false name to use, Rhea had bestowed the name "Minerva" on her. Rhea had been piqued with her family, the Olympians, at the time, so it had seemed delightfully subversive to use the name of a Roman god rather than a Greek one.

If she hadn't been annoyed with her family, she would have used the name "Athena" instead, naming her minion after the goddess of handicrafts and war. Nothing could be more appropriate for a minion who specialized in making costumes for villains.

In any case, Minerva was worth far more to the business than Rhea paid her, and Rhea paid her ten times what most experienced minions were paid. She was loyal, intelligent, and most importantly, she had the valuable power to take drawings and turn them into real-life items.

Two different villains had tried to poach Minerva from her in their first year working together. Thankfully, her minion hadn't looked remotely tempted. But of course, Rhea had had those instigators publicly assassinated anyway. Her employee was hers. If the other villains couldn't command such loyalty or find such talent, it was their own fault for choosing the wrong minions.

And speaking of which . . .

"If you fail the test at the end, you'll be fed to his alligator pit," Rhea announced cheerfully to her students. "Any questions?"

The minions sat bolt upright, their eyes bulging. Any hint of boredom was now replaced by alertness and terror.

Rhea didn't even bother to hide her smirk. That threat was particularly fun because it was true. Granted, their boss had an unfortunate habit of showing mercy after a minion survived for a day and begged, but one could argue that survivors were worth keeping. In any case, it wasn't an efficient method of execution, but Rhea had to admit it had style.

"Good," Rhea said, placing her fingers together and smiling. "Then let's talk about 'the power of love' . . . and how it can be used to your advantage. Take notes, please."

Still looking wild-eyed, the five minions grabbed pens and paper that had been left on the desks in front of them.

Rhea turned to the posters underneath the chalkboard and lifted one up. It was covered in her tidy cursive writing, and the heading on top said *Brainwashing & Hostage-Taking*.

"The most common technique is brainwashing, or hostage-taking," Rhea told her students. "They can be done separately, but they are often done together. Brainwashed friends or boyfriends make an excellent distraction. Sometimes they can even win the battle for you! Look at this example."

She stretched her arms wide to display the image from one of her visions of the past as large as possible. Sights and sounds of a battle appeared translucently in front of her.

A magical girl in a spiked black costume landed on top of her former friend and rammed an ax through her throat. Instead of blood spraying, the magical girl form dissolved into sparkles, and a human girl was left unconscious behind. The brainwashed friend leapt up into the air and took off.

Two of the minions leaned forward eagerly, bloodlust clear in their eyes.

Good sign, Rhea approved. *They might die early if they're eager for battle and aren't smart about it, but that level of viciousness can also be a motivation to become great. Much better than apathy.*

Rhea ended the scene, neglecting to show that the brainwashed magical girl's sister had become a magical girl a few days later, then chased after the brainwashed girl and saved her. She'd said *battle,* not *war.*

"Obviously, however, brainwashing is brittle and breaks easily," Rhea continued. "If you choose someone who has no powers, such as a friend or family member, it might be wise to keep that person as a mere hostage who has no motivation to escape, rather than giving them power and sending them to fight in your war."

One of the minions slumped low in his chair, looking bored. Rhea snapped her fingers together, miming alligator teeth, and he hurriedly sat up straight.

"Just remember that sometimes hostage situations can backfire and cause power-ups," Rhea continued. "Magical girls tend to spontaneously develop new powers when under stress."

She pointed at one of the subheadings on the poster, which she read aloud.

"Never make a brainwashed boyfriend attack a magical girl unless you're an idiot. That *will* cause a power-up, and it *often* results in the death of the minion involved. Far better to choose people the magical girl doesn't want to hurt but isn't desperately attached to, such as random classmates."

The minions scribbled this down.

"And finally: never, *ever* turn your back on an unwilling ally. Brainwashing has a tendency to suddenly break at the most inconvenient possible moment for you."

While her students took notes, Rhea lifted up the second poster, which had the heading *Infiltration* on top. She put it on the board in front of the first one.

"Now, infiltration requires more subtlety. Many times, a better option than brainwashing a civilian is to pretend to be a civilian yourself, then betray your enemy at the worst possible moment. Write down the following phrase: 'I'm a new transfer student.' You will need to practice that one hundred times until you can keep a straight face while saying it."

Three of the minions looked dubious, but they all wrote down something.

"Also, this sounds counterintuitive, but remember to go out of your way to *offend* a magical girl the first time she meets you," Rhea continued. "For some reason, this often works to make a magical girl fall in love with you when you start acting nice later. It's not known why this is, but it's thought that if you can get her to hate you at the start, it's much easier to make her love you because she already feels strongly about you."

All five of the minions looked dubious.

"I know it sounds ludicrous," Rhea agreed, "but it works. Write it down. If you can turn out to be 'really' sensitive and angsty later, all the better. Mysteriousness always helps, and it is absolutely essential that you be incredibly attractive."

She didn't mention any of the more advanced tactics, such as brainwashing a few girls to set up a fan club and act jealous.

"So, if you show strong acting skills in your first year or two of employment, and you are plausibly young enough to play the part of a romantic interest, you might receive the joyful news that you've been chosen for an undercover assignment! If that happens, congratulations! It will pay very well if you complete it successfully!"

Unfortunately, undercover jobs like that also had a very high rate of minions falling in love with the girls for real and being "redeemed," which was why Rhea tended to despise that tactic. Still, their boss had insisted she include it, so she was.

"Due to that fact, sometime in the future, your boss may require you to dress up like a teenager and seduce or befriend — *why aren't you taking notes?!*"

Scribble scribble scribble scribble.

"Better." Rhea smirked with gleeful malice. "Now, on to my personal favorite technique: *Corruption.*"

She was about to reach for the third poster and begin an overview, but the door burst open, and Minerva stood panting behind it.

"Ma'am, your three o'clock appointment is demanding to see you an hour early. Something about a magical girl costume?"

"Ah! My favorite technique in action!" Rhea beamed at the news. She was annoyed to be interrupted in the middle of her lesson, but she'd been looking forward to this appointment for awhile. That customer was one of the most disgustingly spoiled little girls she'd ever met, which made the child a perfect target. "Minerva, will you substitute teach?"

Her minion dove for the fourth poster before the sentence was even finished. "Love to!"

The poster had the heading *Alligator Pit Survival Tips.*

Yelps of terror rose up as Rhea shut the door and headed downstairs.

It was a shame the spoiled little girl's mother had come to the store with her, but not a surprise. You could hardly expect a seven-year-old to enter a fashion boutique on her own.

The Lecture

"Hello," Rhea said smoothly, descending from the last stair and stepping onto the sales floor. "How can I help you today?"

The little girl had chin-length hair and a headband, and was wearing a sweet little dress with ruffles and lace. The mother was tall and unnaturally skinny, with very short, slicked back hair, enameled fingernails, and a highly suggestive dress that was the height of Paris fashion this year. Her perfectly sculpted eyebrows were drawn together in an impatient scowl.

"Joanie has decided on her costume," the woman declared in an imperious tone. "We demand you make it today."

Rhea was immediately rubbed the wrong way. *Five weeks being indecisive, then you want it done in one day. Grr!*

But she hid her irritation. She had a reputation for speed, after all. It was one of the reasons she charged a premium over most designers. That speed was, of course, due to her indispensable minion's power to magically make clothes out of drawings.

"Glad to hear it!" she replied with a smile. "Shall we start sketching the basic concepts?"

She already knew the direction she wanted to push them in. Pale blue would be most flattering for the little girl's complexion, though lilac or green would be acceptable. An animal motif would be ideal, perhaps a puppy or a kitten. Those could easily be morphed to wolf or tiger for a dark form . . .

"Won't be necessary," the woman announced, whipping a folded-up piece of paper out from behind her back. "Joanie already designed it."

Rhea stumbled in horror at the sketch. It was a dress that seemed to have three different motifs going, all of them clashing.

"Um," Rhea said, gasping for breath. "Yes, that's . . . that's lovely. Let's just —"

"Then Mummy found the most perfectist fabric!" the child beamed, pulling out an armful of flourescent pink from a bag beside her mother's feet.

"But that's . . . *acetate,*" Rhea managed, feeling like she was about to faint. "It's hideous. And it dissolves on contact with nail polish remover. I have a lovely robin egg blue sateen that —"

"Hear that, Joanie?" the woman directed, shaking her finger at the little girl. "No wearing nail polish with it."

The little girl's eyes welled up in tears. "But I *want* to, Mummy!"

Stupid, spoiled brat . . .

"Well, let's play with a few refinements, shall we?" Rhea said in a friendly tone, recovering her composure. This wouldn't be the first client who, despite paying a lot of money for a designer, developed the ludicrous idea that Rhea was a seamstress who would take their terrible design and make it for them.

Usually a few "refinements" were all it took to change a mind-numbingly dreadful design into something closer to what Rhea had intended in the first place. And customers with more money than sense did tend to be valuable sources of revenue. The mother seemed the type who wouldn't check to see if they'd been "accidentally" double-charged.

These nightmare customers were resistant to any attempts at improvement, however. As Rhea sat at her public drawing desk, the one near the entrance, the mother and daughter surrounded her on both sides and made running commentaries about every line her pencil made.

"No."

"No."

"Not girly enough."

"It hasta be pretty."

"Needs ruffles right there."

"I wanna have lace!"

"No, not lace right there. Put it right there."

"More lace!"

"Is that a dart or a zipper?"

"I wanna have zippers!"

"Make it a zipper."

"More zippers!"

"And zippers there and there, too. Lots of zippers."

"More lace!"

The result was an atrocity of epic proportions. It was *worse* than the original design, to Rhea's horror.

"Perfect!" the mother declared. "How much?"

You mean, how much do I want to feed you to an alligator pit?!

Through clenched teeth, Rhea named a sum that was ten times higher than usual. The woman went to the cash register without blinking. Steaming in fury, Rhea charged quadruple the amount she'd quoted, but the woman seemed to neither notice nor care.

Hate hate hate hate —

"Get it done in an hour!" the woman called, waving as she steered her daughter out of the shop. "We'll be back for it then!"

Rhea nearly choked on her rage. An *hour?* Did she even think that was *possible?* The rush fee clearly stated "within 24 hours"!

Yes, she had Minerva. Yes, it was technically possible. But just being able to look at the appalling result without sobbing would take hours on its own. And as for designing a cooler version of that costume for a dark form . . .!

They'd left the bag filled with atrocious cloth behind. So there was not even an excuse to try to salvage the zippered, fluffy, bow-encrusted ballgown with a different fabric instead.

Rhea seized the bag and stormed up the stairs.

She threw open the door to her upstairs classroom in time to hear the tail end of Minerva's enthusiastic story about the last student to fail Rhea's class. The newbie minions were paralyzed in terror. They weren't even taking notes.

Minerva waved her arms excitedly. "Now, the thing you want to remember about alligator teeth . . ."

Rhea dropped the bag of fabric on the ground. She flung the sketch down on top of it.

"Make this out of that fabric," she said.

Minerva turned around slowly, clearly disappointed to be required to go back to work. Then she caught sight of the cloth. Horror rose on her face.

"But that's . . . *acetate.*"

"I know."

"But it's acetate!"

"Do it anyway."

"But it's —!"

"I charged her the Ultra-Special Tier A customer rate. You'll get your usual commission."

Minerva reluctantly leaned forward to pick up the sketch. Then she saw the contents and let out a scream, dropping it.

"I know," Rhea said grimly. "Do it anyway."

"But it's —! It's —!"

"Do it anyway."

"But it's *that!!*"

"I also quadruple-charged it."

"But, boss, don't you know what'll happen to your reputation?" Minerva asked frantically. "The customer will tell everyone it's a Rhea Korstanos original. What if everyone laughs at you? What if they *don't* laugh at you?" Minerva was hyperventilating. "What if we have to make more of these?!"

"If we do, we'll hold our noses and promote those dresses as the latest fashion," Rhea said coolly. It was a dreadful thought, but fads were easily displaced, especially when they were clearly ugly. An idea occurred to her, and a sneaky smile spread across her face. "That would certainly make it easier to promote the idea that villains look cooler . . ."

"Or all your magical girl customers will just go to other designers!" Minerva exclaimed.

The smile dropped from Rhea's face.

Minerva was right. Of course Minerva was right. What was she thinking? She couldn't let a customer go out in public in that atrocity and claim Rhea Korstanos had designed it.

But how could she get out of it at this point? She'd already charged the money. The customers would be back in an hour.

"What's acetate?" one of the minions asked, leaning forward.

"The worst fabric in the world to wear," Minerva moaned.

Of course. Rhea relaxed, and a smile spread across her face. *There's a very simple solution to this.*

"Make the dress out of that fabric," Rhea ordered Minerva. "Make sure every last scrap of it is made out of acetate. Even the fabric of the zippers. *Especially* the fabric of the zippers. And use the flimsiest plastic possible for the zipper teeth."

"You're gonna claim it fell apart?" Minerva asked with a grin.

"Nothing so crude," Rhea sniffed. "I can't have my brand linked with shoddy workmanship. No, there will be a terrible stroke of bad luck that has nothing to do with me."

"Which is what?"

Rhea left the room. She came back with a pair of squirt guns that she'd confiscated from a pair of rowdy little boys inside her store a few weeks ago. Last time she'd checked, those two brats were still wondering where they'd mislaid their toys.

"Who wants a guarantee that they won't end up in the alligator pit?"

Five students' hands immediately raised.

"Very well." Rhea handed the toys to her minion. "Extra credit to anyone who fills these squirt guns with nail polisher remover and attacks them. Make sure to give the acetate a good, thorough soaking. I'll make them a 'new one' that doesn't even slightly resemble the old one as a free gift when they come back to complain that the girl's costume dissolved."

And she smiled, baring her teeth just like an alligator.

There was always a solution when there were people to manipulate into doing your will.

Chapter 3
The Proposal

Welcome to Mágico!" An elegant, brown-skinned woman stood up from what looked like a throne as they entered the president's receiving room. "I am Presidente Eloise Santos. Are you Florence Atkins?"

Florence gulped and nodded. The room looked way more ostentatious than she had expected. It was empty and cavernous and had . . . columns. Lots and lots of columns.

"Y-yes . . ." Florence said quickly. Her voice echoed in the vast hollow space. "I'm here about . . . making a government for magical girls . . ."

"Of course you are; that's why I sent for you," the woman said briskly. Her clothing resembled a cross between a magical girl costume and a business suit, and despite her skin being brown, her eyes were bright green. "So, what's your proposal?"

For a moment, Florence was struck dumb. "P-proposal?"

"Well, I assume you have a proposal," the woman said coldly, glancing down at her fingernails, as if bored. "Or are you just wasting my time?"

"I am *not* wasting your time!" Florence said furiously.

"Good." The woman smirked, looking back up at her again. "Then let's hear your proposal."

Florence gulped. "O-okay. Well, the reason I'm here is to discuss the Sonnenkinder Government. The thing about the Sonnenkinder Government —"

"Call it a union," the woman interrupted, sitting back on the throne with her legs crossed. That informality, in this room, was more than a little jarring. "Other governments are less likely to feel threatened by it that way. I learned that the hard way when my attempt didn't get off the ground."

"Fine," Florence said, a little annoyed. "The thing about the Sonnenkinder Union —"

"Oh, and avoid the German term," the woman added. "It sounds pretentious, and I assume you don't speak the language. Try English instead."

"'Sonnenkinder' *was* borrowed into English!"

"Maybe it was in American English," the woman shrugged. "It wasn't in Australian English, which is the international standard. Try again."

"Okay. The thing about the —"

"Oh, and stop repeating yourself. It's not very persuasive."

"Stop criticizing everything!" Florence said angrily. "At least let me finish a sentence first!"

"I criticize because I know what I am talking about," the woman said coolly. "Do you?"

Intimidation radiated off of the throne. Suddenly the woman seemed like an authority figure again.

Florence swallowed. "Well . . . I've researched . . ."

"That's a 'no,' then." The woman snorted, folding her arms. "Which makes me wonder . . . do you actually understand the cost of what you're saying you want to do?"

"I know it'll take work!" Florence said quickly. "I'm willing —"

"Clearly you don't." The woman sighed loudly. "This is the problem with working with magical girls. I swear I wasn't this clueless when I ran for president. Let's start with the obvious, then. To run something this extensive, you would no longer have time for schooling."

Huh? Florence thought blankly. *Who said I'll be running it?*

"Now, hang on a second!" Florence's dad cried, his eyebrows drawn in anger. "You can't ask her to quit school! She's only sixteen!"

"Five years ago, when I was her age, I led a revolutionary battalion," Eloise Santos said. "There is no 'only sixteen' to me."

"I never said I wanted to *run* it!" Florence added. "I just want to see that it gets started!"

The woman stared at her, unblinking. "If not you, then who? Are you really saying that you want to start a government and then have nothing to do with making sure it works properly? That seems terribly irresponsible."

Florence faltered. "Well . . . I mean . . . I know I'm not qualified . . ."

"Nobody's qualified for what you want to do," the president said flatly. "Nobody's done it before. I've looked into you. You're the magical girl Pink Dragon. You volunteered for a year as an FBI aide. You placed sixth in a Magical Girl Team of the Year competition. You came here because you care enough about this to be motivated to see it done right. It seems to me you're the most qualified anyone's going to get short of being an actual politician, and I can't do it because nobody will trust it if the president of one particular country is running it."

It felt like a gaping chasm had opened up where Florence's stomach used to be. Her mouth was dry.

"So, Florence Atkins, let's be totally honest with each other," Eloise Santos said, leaning forward and staring at her with those shockingly green eyes. "I want to see this happen, but I won't have it be bungled. I agree that it's needed. I tried to start something similar myself, and it didn't work because I didn't have enough support at the time. So I'm willing to lend you my backing. But only if you're absolutely serious about it. Are you?"

Silence stretched across the vast room. In the silence, Florence could hear the echoes of her own breathing.

"You want me to be a . . . a leader?" Florence asked, her voice cracking. "I've never led anything. Kendra — my best friend — she was always the one in charge."

"And how did that end?" the woman asked.

"She turned villain," Florence said in a low voice.

"Well, I'm glad you're willing to admit it," the president said, nodding sharply. "I, of course, learned that when I looked up the information about you. And I won't be the only person to notice that connection. Many will ask why someone who is friends with a villain would want to be in a position of authority. Some might whisper that she is the reason you're doing this, to undermine the community and give strength to the villains."

"Kendra *is* the reason I'm doing this, and it's the exact opposite of that!" Florence flared. "I don't want any more magical girls turning into villains because the laws are so lax that they wind up crossing the line without even realizing it! I want a magical girl government to prevent people like Kendra ever happening again!"

A smile curled on the president's lips. "That is an excellent answer. Nicely delivered. Remember to keep the same vehemence when asked in an interview. Well, then, let me be clear with you. Good leaders rarely receive glory. They often make great sacrifices. They're usually criticized, infrequently thanked. And if you want this organization to happen, you're going to have to become a leader, make no mistake. So?"

"That's a lot to ask a teenager to do," Florence's dad objected before Florence could speak.

Eloise Santos shrugged. "I'm not asking her to do it. She is asking *me* to help her do it. And if she really wants to do this, she will have to deal with all of that, regardless of age. So?"

Florence inhaled deeply.

Did she really want to do that? Become a leader? Take charge of a massive international organization that she had no qualifications to run and that might crash and burn utterly? She wasn't so sure she did.

But if she didn't . . . who would?

Surely there were others who could do it better.

But if so . . . why hadn't anyone else started it already?

And she wanted it to exist. For Kendra's sake, and for the sake of all other magical girls out there who were close to becoming like her.

"I want to do this," Florence said, her voice shaking a little. "I know I haven't got experience yet, but . . . I really want to."

"And you desire my backing?" the woman asked.

"Yes."

"Suppose you *fail?*" The woman's eyes were fierce.

Florence gulped. "I'll try really hard not to?"

"Huh." The expression softened. "Well, if nothing else, I like your humility. That'll make you capable of learning all the things you don't know. Okay, Florence Atkins. I might take a chance on you. I think you'll do. Show me your magical girl form, so I can see whether you look authoritative enough for a press conference without makeup and wardrobe added."

"Uh . . ." Florence said.

"She hasn't been able to transform since her bracelet —" Florence's mother began.

"We're not sure what's —" Florence's father added.

Eloise Santos drew back. "You don't *have* one?!"

"I did!" Florence said rapidly. "I didn't quit or anything!" Suddenly, she was glad that was true. "But something happened to my focus item five weeks ago —"

As quickly as possible, she explained the situation. The twelve mysterious gemstones, the lack of ability to transform —

"Oh," Eloise Santos said. She seemed on the verge of rolling her eyes. "It mutated. That's not uncommon."

"But it's more than that!" Florence exclaimed. "Just look! Pink Dragon . . . *flare!*"

She summoned the bracelet in a roar of fire. As always, it appeared on her arm when she called it, but it did nothing else. And nothing else happened.

"My transformation words don't work anymore!" she cried. "I can't transform, or use my powers, or —"

"Have you tried choosing a new name?"

"New name?" Florence stared at the woman blankly.

"Sure. Power-ups sometimes require name shifts."

"But I've powered up before — that didn't happen!"

"Have you dealt with any lifestyle changes since then?"

"Well . . . yes . . ." Florence hesitated. "Kendra turned villain and Felicity quit, so I lost my whole team . . ."

"There you are," Eloise Santos said. "Your magic wants a new name. Choose one, and you'll be fine."

She waited with an air of expectation, and Florence realized she meant *right now.*

"I can't — I can't just make up a new name like that!" Florence sputtered. "It took me months the first time!"

"You were Pink Dragon, right? Try a different color."

A different color? Well, that might make sense. She hadn't wanted to wear pink anymore . . .

"Crimson Dragon . . . *flare!*"

Nothing happened.

"Why didn't it work?!" Florence exclaimed.

The president shrugged. "Clearly you want more than a name shift. Did you picture the way you want your new magical girl form to look, what kind of powers you want it to have?"

"Magic fills that stuff in, doesn't it?"

"It does if you know on some level what you want, yes."

Florence's mind went blank. "I . . . I figured I'd find out what I wanted when I transformed. I'd see my magical girl form, and I'd know, 'Oh, that's what I wanted all along!'"

The president of Mágico snorted. "Magic's not a shortcut to psychoanalysis. If you don't know what you want, the magic system won't know what you want, either. Try picturing your new costume and powers, and see how that works."

Florence closed her eyes and imagined, but nothing she came up with seemed right. Every idea she had of what magical girls should look like came from Kendra, and she didn't want her magical girl form to be influenced by Kendra. Not after what Kendra had become. The more she thought about it, the more she didn't even like the name "Crimson Dragon." It was too much a continuation of the naming pattern of the Wings of Justice.

And as for powers . . . how was she supposed to know what kind of powers were most useful for a solo magical girl? She'd never been a solo magical girl before.

"I'm sorry," Florence said, biting her lip. "If it's a dealbreaker for me to not have a magical girl form right now, then that's that. The only thing I'm sure I want right now is what I told you about. I have no idea what kind of magic I want, or even *whether* I still want it."

The woman frowned, staring at her for a long time.

"All right," she said at last, reaching down into the side of her throne and coming up with a sheet of paper and a pen. "We'll just have to adjust. The press conference will need to show at least one impressive magical girl as a founder, or nobody will take it seriously. If you aren't that magical girl, you'll need to have several behind you to make up for that fact. Let's say three."

She scribbled on the paper.

"As for your own magical girl form, make figuring out what you want for it a priority. Forget that question of 'whether.' The answer is yes. You're a leader of magical girls, not a sports team. You need magic to do that job. I want you to unveil your new magical girl form at the opening ceremonies. Are we agreed?"

"Um . . ."

The president seemed to take this as an assent. "I can think of at least twenty girls we would be wise to invite early on. You'll want at least three of them as founding members. Do you have any opinions about which ones you want?"

Lentswe Counterpoint, Florence thought immediately, but she wouldn't dare approach her favorite singer. Besides, that South African magical girl had to be busy with all the anti-apartheid protests she kept organizing.

"Um . . . Princesa?" Florence asked hesitantly. That was a famous magical girl actress in Peru. "Edelweiss?" A famous singing magical girl in Austria. "La Rama Fragrante?" A famous healing magical girl in Argentina.

Eloise Santos did not look impressed with her choices. "None of those were even on my list. We can invite them later, if you wish, but not as founding members. Princesa's controversial, Edelweiss is quiet, and La Rama Fragrante is insistently apolitical. None of them will influence people to join the movement."

"O-oh," Florence said.

"I'll tell you what, Florence Atkins," the president said briskly. "I'll choose the three best options for you. I'm not the only person you should speak to and convince about this. Talk with these three magical girls. We'll move forward if they agree with you."

She struck out line after line on the piece of paper. Then she held it out.

Florence swallowed and walked over and took it.

There were, indeed, about twenty names written on there, and most of them now had a line through them. Only three remained.

Chung-Ae, of the Righteous Army.
Snowbelle, in Antarctica.
Dulcina, in Mexico City.

Florence swallowed. She knew who two of those were. One was a resistance leader against Japanese occupation, and one was considered a criminal and impossible to find. She'd never heard of the third.

"If they all agree," Eloise Santos told her, "I'll know you have the ability to persuade enough influential people from different viewpoints to support your cause to make it a success. Come back when you have all three."

Goosebumps rose on Florence's skin. "How am I supposed to go to all those places?"

"Oh, I'll provide my private jet. And I'll forewarn Chung-Ae you're coming so the Righteous Army will let you into their base. You'll do the rest."

Florence gave her parents a panicked look.

"I'm not sure I'm okay with this," Florence's mother said.

"I'm not sure it's our decision," Florence's father sighed. "We said we'd support her with whatever she needs. We can't back out of that now."

"But she's only sixteen."

"You heard what the president did when *she* was sixteen."

"Florence isn't her!"

"But if she wants to be like her, it's her decision."

Florence's parents both stared at her intently.

Florence squirmed uncomfortably. If her parents had refused, that would have made this easy. She could have gotten out of it and then relaxed into her normal life, complaining all the while that her parents had stood in her way. Why were they making her go through with this? It was much easier if you didn't have to follow through with the things you said you believed!

Florence closed her eyes and breathed in deeply.

Do I want to make excuses, or do I want to do what needs to be done?

She was *mad* that nobody was taking this terrible burden off her, but if nobody else was going to do it, well, she had to.

No matter what it cost her.

"I'm going," Florence said. She managed to keep her voice from shaking. "Will you both come with me?"

"Do you want us to?" Florence's mom looked startled.

"Yeah. I'd love the moral support. If . . ." She looked at the president hesitantly. "If that's allowed?"

"Sure." Presidente Santos shrugged. "If they're helpful, that just means you're using available resources effectively."

"Then we'll come," Florence's father said. He glanced at his wife. "Of course, we'll need to call Jacob . . ."

Florence barely suppressed a giggle. Her little brother was going to be furious to find out he was missing a trip around the world. He'd insisted on spending the night at his best friend's house instead of coming with them to Mágico, because *"that dumb meeting sounds super boring."* Honestly, she was glad they wouldn't be bringing him. It would probably work much better not to have him there.

Florence turned to face the president of Mágico and squared her shoulders.

"I won't let you down," she declared.

Presidente Santos smiled. "I hope not. Good luck to you."

Chapter 4
The Dissension

The phone bounced off the wall with a satisfying *SLAM!*

"Minerva!" Rhea's voice shouted from upstairs. "I need you to make a new phone! The old one is broken!"

Zazz sighed and rolled her eyes. She put down the inventory she was organizing and checked to make sure the front door of the store was locked and the curtains were drawn. Then she unwrapped her tail from her leg and headed upstairs.

"Yes?" she asked, not entirely politely, leaning against the doorway to her boss's upstairs workroom as she folded her arms.

"Here," Rhea said, flinging a piece of paper at her.

Zazz caught the paper. She peeled the image off it, and it inflated into a three-dimensional object as she did so.

"Thank you," Rhea said. Then she turned and flung the new phone at the wall. "Stuck-up, self-centered, short-sighted —!"

"Ah," Zazz said. There was only one type of person who could affect her boss this strongly. "Your family again."

Rhea's fists clenched. "I am NOT WEAK, Minerva!"

Duh? Zazz thought. "Of course you're not. You're subtle. There's a difference."

"Try telling THEM that!" Rhea gestured at the two shattered phones. "Go on! Make a new one and tell them that!"

"Yeah, no thanks," Zazz said. "Wouldn't do any good, boss. I've tried telling my family the same thing about me, remember?"

Zazz came from an old, established family of grand artists in her home world. Back home, a magical ability like hers was common enough that it was only considered useful if you drew beautiful things to create. And she had no drawing ability whatsoever.

Rhea had seen the potential of her powers when nobody else had. She'd been the first person to ever treat Zazz with respect. That was the reason Zazz was fiercely loyal to her.

Of course, it didn't hurt that the boss paid well, and the other offers Zazz had gotten from the boss's rivals were insultingly low. Seriously, what did they think she was, a low-level mook?

The one thing Zazz didn't like about her boss was when she got all moody after making a report to her family. Why didn't she just stop reporting to them if they always treated her that way? Zazz hadn't talked to anyone in her home world since coming here.

"You'd think they'd see that I'm a unique asset, wouldn't you?" Rhea ranted. "But no! They called me 'weak' and 'worthless.' Half their victories owe everything to my groundwork! Why don't they *understand* that?!"

"Because they're idiots," Zazz shrugged. "Why do you care? You don't need them. You're better than that."

"I can't get born mages at their proper place on top of the world if the other born mages won't help me," Rhea fumed. "And I want the Olympians on top of all villains, not the Deathwaves!"

Ah. Zazz snorted. She didn't understand the concept of family loyalty at all. As far as she was concerned, this obsession with putting her family on top was her boss's only weakness.

"This is the third time I've tried to report what Chronos is doing," Rhea snarled, her fists clenching. "Have they listened to me once? No! In fact, Great-Uncle Nico had the nerve to get on himself and tell me it sounds like she's being more useful than I am!"

"Maybe you should do something yourself," Zazz said.

"Maybe it's their duty to do something themselves," Rhea shot back. "She's a traitor to the *family,* not me. Besides, what exactly am I supposed to do? I can't track her movements!"

The Dissension

You could hire an army of assassins, Zazz thought. *You know where she lives, right?* But she knew better than to suggest it. She'd tried that before, and Rhea had gone off on some long rant about how that wouldn't help because she couldn't spy on the defenses in any area Chronos was currently in, and her sister had a teleportation device and could just sneak off somewhere else, and . . .

Yeah, yeah, yeah. It was pretty obvious the boss just didn't want to kill her sister. It was that family loyalty thing again.

Okay, maybe it made sense from a tactical perspective to try to convert someone with useful powers like seeing the future over to their side. But seriously, even though the woman was a sucker about everything else, she didn't seem to be convertible about that. In which case, they really just ought to cut their losses and send an overwhelming force to kill her.

Well, except for the teleportation device and the fact that Rhea's sister didn't mind being a hermit and ignoring people for a decade. That would make it really hard to find her again if she escaped, so they'd have a hidden enemy who was highly motivated to kill them both. But still. If the woman was a liability, why not at *least* send somebody to execute the magical girl who was doing her bidding? And frame somebody else for that?

Wait . . . she wants the Olympians to do that, doesn't she? Zazz realized, her eyes narrowing. *Then the boss could convince her sister to join her side in revenge against the head of the family, their common enemy, and they'd wind up allies forever.*

That was a pretty good plan, all things considered. The boss's sister was definitely naive enough to fall for an obvious approach like that. And Zazz could applaud the boss's willingness to sell out the head of her family. He was definitely an enemy.

There was just one little problem, which was that the boss's Great-Uncle Nico seemed to be either too stupid to see that Chronos was a problem, or too smart to play the role Rhea intended for him.

"I believe they resent that you quit blackmailing convenient politicians for them, ma'am," Zazz said. "Maybe, if you start doing that again . . ."

"Blackmail . . ." Rhea murmured. A slow smile spread across her face. "They want *blackmail,* do they?"

Zazz suddenly had terrible misgivings. The boss looked way too happy. "Um, I'm not so sure you should . . ."

Rhea smirked and waved a hand to dismiss her. "What's the head of the family been up to lately?"

From down the hallway, Nico heard two voices talking.

"I'm sorry, but I can't let you in." It was Apollo, one of his many grandsons. The boy was a fool, but his barrier power made him a useful guard. "Grandfather says —"

"Oh, really?" a woman's voice asked. "Would you like your wife to see *this?*"

A yelp of horror later, there were footsteps in heeled boots clomping down the hallway.

Nico cursed to himself. Had the boy been cheating on his wife again? Trust that blasted woman to be able to find the one weakness in his defenses and shove her way through.

He arranged the mirror on his desk to point back at the doorway so that he could see his visitor clearly without turning around. Then the door opened.

"Hello, Great-Uncle Nico," Rhea said pleasantly. She stepped no further than the doorway, folding her arms. "It's high time you listened to me."

Nico didn't turn around. He raised his finger and activated his ranged touch-of-death power, which sparked from his finger in an ominous cloud. "You realize I have the ability to cause instant death to people who bother me."

"Oh, yes, I realize that," Rhea said cheerfully. "I also realize that you've lost vision in one eye and have no more depth perception. What an interesting secret to be keeping from the rest of the family."

Nico cursed under his breath. The worst part about running a villain family was that there were always young upstarts waiting to pounce and take advantage of any weaknesses from age.

"I can aim it through the mirror just fine," he growled. "Look at my past if you don't believe me."

"Oh, I have. I know you can do that." She smirked. "But not from this far away. I know your aim stinks."

He flung his power through the mirror. It rebounded and zoomed towards the blasted woman. She, unfortunately, took one step to the side and evaded it. It exploded against the wall behind her, leaving a smoking black hole.

"Now, turn around and listen to me," she said. "We need to discuss the problem with my sister."

"There is no problem with her!" Nico barked. "How many times do I have to tell you? The fact that she's finally doing something at all is cause for celebration! Unlike *you*, who refused to get that bill passed in parliament to make villains legal!"

"Because it would have been short-sighted!" Rhea returned. "If you make a government too corrupt, the people catch on and revolt! Then we'd lose all our power to manipulate things behind the scenes!"

"Do you know how much *power* that would have given us?! We could have openly ruled!"

"Yes! Until the magical girls converged on the Olympians from every other nation and smashed the family into oblivion! You can't rule openly until you've crushed all opposition *first!* Which is exactly what I told you back then!"

"We are descended from gods!" Nico roared. "It is our manifest destiny to rule as our ancestors once did!"

"*Yes!*" Rhea yelled. "So let's be smart about it, so we don't get defeated like they did!"

Nico snarled at the blatant blasphemy. She knew the family had only declined because of the will of the Fates, and that it was the will of the Fates for them to rise again.

That was why they had been getting steadily more powerful over the past century. That was why they had more powerful born mages now than they had since the days of Ouranos, the original head of the family. That was why they were posed at the brink of greatness, and needed only to reach out and take it.

How dare she imply that any human hand had ever brought their ancestors down?

How dare she imply that any human hand ever might again?

No doubt, if asked, the woman would sneer that she could see the past, so of course she knew the truth about the family better than everyone else.

But Rhea was a smooth-tongued liar. She would say anything to further her current agenda. It was one of the reasons he did not trust her, and he never would. Her word was too easily faked, her lies believable, her truths slippery.

Her sister Chronos, by contrast, had always been far more convenient. Easily led, stupidly dense, and blindly honest. If Rhea hadn't poisoned the kid against the whole family through her backstabbing attempts to make Chronos loyal to her rather than Nico, she would have made a perfect minion.

Yes, the family's losing access to that future-seeing power was all Rhea's fault. The family's losing access to that docile, naive lackey was all Rhea's doing.

He would never forgive her for that.

Nico had no concerns about Chronos. All the things her little minion named Seraph was now doing seemed like typical villain activities, and he knew the twit lacked the wits to be setting up anything more subtle than that. Rhea, on the other hand, was a known liar who had already tried to wrest control of the family away from him once. That was why he had exiled her.

Useful power or not, he really should have killed her instead.

"Your attempts to use your sister as bait for my attention are charming," Nico sneered, "but I am not as stupid as you seem to think. You want me to reinstate you in the family by using her as a common enemy. Then you want to sneak around and turn the rest of them against me. Unfortunately for you, I know you, and I can see through exactly what you're doing. There is no threat. Chronos lacks the brains to be a threat to anyone. This is just a power play."

"You're a fool if you think that's true. Turn around."

"Absolutely not! I will not humor your power play!"

"I wouldn't make up something this important as part of a *power play!* Chronos is an imminent threat to magical girl corruption, and without magical girls becoming so corrupt that the world turns on them, we stand no chance of ruling! If we don't stop her, it might take decades to undo the work she and her minions are doing! Now I *demand* you listen to me!"

"Your credibility was shot six years ago, when you tried to supplant me," Nico laughed. He raised his finger, activating his power, and a cloud of smoke and sparks rose. He also pushed the button on his desk to summon his elite guards. "Now get out. I am calling security."

Rhea stood her ground, not moving an inch. "You know, the funny thing about your *security* . . ."

Armored elite security ninjas flipped down from the ceiling, wielding guns and wands and more exotic weapons.

BLAM!

". . . Is that most were happy to switch their allegiance to me."

Rhea smirked as she looked down at the corpse of her Great-Uncle Nico.

The ninjas slid back into the ceiling, and Rhea walked over to her great-uncle's desk. She kicked his corpse to the side and picked up the phone from his desk. Then she flopped onto the couch at the back of the room.

"Minerva?" she said into the phone. "Mm-hm, yeah, he's dead. I *told* you not to worry."

"Who's going to run the family now, boss?"

What a silly question.

"Me." Rhea examined her fingernails. She seemed to have chipped the paint on one of the pinkies, more's the pity. It must have happened when she'd crawled through the secret passages to talk to the security team this morning. "I hope you don't think I'd trust anyone else with the position. Do me a favor and close my shop for the next two weeks? We're going to be very busy."

The family needed a fresh start. And that corpse on the floor was no longer standing in the way.

It was time to bring the Olympians back to glory.